The Grapes Grow Sweet

This book is a gift for

Sonoma Mountain

from

Ms. Kelley's class
1998 - 99

The Grapes Grow Sweet

A Child's First Harvest in Wine Country

Story and Illustrations by
Lynne Tuft

Text by
Tessa DeCarlo

STUDIO 8 / RIVER PRESS
Napa, California

All summer long Julian has been watching the grapes on the vines that grow all around his house. All summer long Julian has been waiting for the harvest, because this year he is big enough to help.

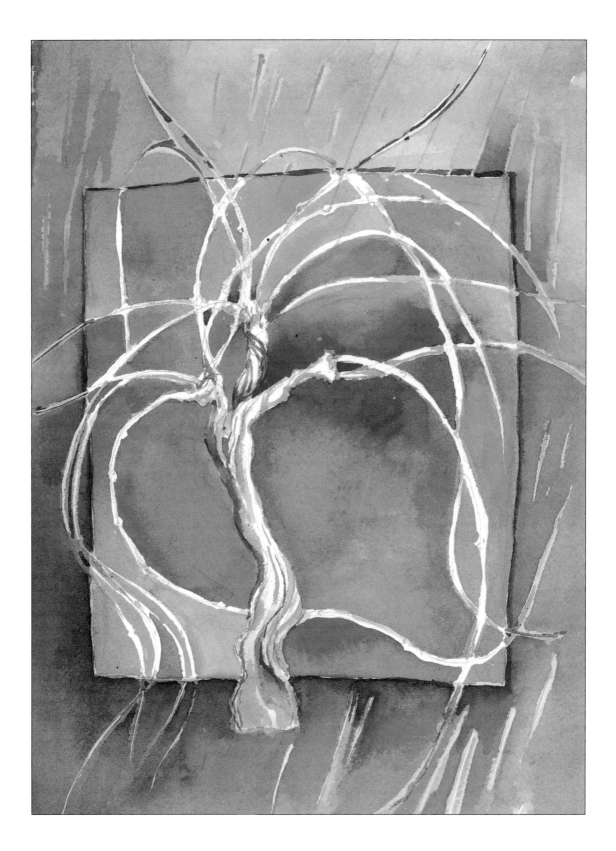

In the winter the vines were bare and gray, fast asleep under the cold winter rain.

In the spring the new leaves opened to the sun and the vines' tiny flowers bloomed.

Then one day Julian found baby
grapes hiding among the pale green
leaves, smaller than his sister
Jenna's littlest fingernail.

Now the leaves are so thick that when Julian and Jenna play hide-and-seek in the vineyard, Julian's mother can hardly find them, and the grapes hang in heavy clusters, each one big as the end of Julian's thumb and dark as the night sky.

All summer long Julian has been tasting. At first the grapes were so sour they puckered his tongue, but little by little the long hot days are filling them with sugar.

"When they have a little more sugar, it'll be time to pick," says Julian's father. "The grapes have to be sweet for the wine to be good."

One day they are sweet as jam. "Almost there," Julian's mother says. "Any day now."

Then one night Julian hears voices in the vineyard and a rumbling like thunder. "The gondolas are here!" he yells.

Julian and his father go out in the dark to see the gondolas lined up, huge and empty. "Tomorrow the harvest starts," Julian's father says. "One week for us to finish a whole year's work."

The next morning Julian and his mother get up while the sky is still dark as sleep. The tractor starts up with a roar that sends frightened birds racketing out of the trees.

At the old barn, Lorenzo, his wife and their crew are waiting. They talk and laugh and sharpen their grape-picking knives. In the winter they were here to cut back the sleeping vines. They came again in the spring to tie up the new vine shoots. Now they are going to help Julian's family pick the grapes.

"Look who's here!" Lorenzo cries. "You're growing faster than a vine shoot, *amigito.* Getting so big I almost didn't recognize you."

Julian helps his mother drive the rattling, roaring tractor, pulling the first gondola out to where the crew is working.

Then it is as if someone has turned up the speed on the day
that has hardly even begun yet. For the harvest is a race—a race
to get the grapes into the gondolas as fast as the pickers can
pick. Then a man named Mac will come in his truck to haul the
gondolas off to the winery, quick before the hot sun can make
the grapes' sweetness start to spoil.

Lorenzo and the others sing and shout as they work, cutting grapes off the vines with their sharp, curved knives. The pickers run to dump their bins of grapes into the gondola and run back to pick more.

Julian finds
one perfect bunch
that has fallen onto
the ground.

He picks a grape
and tastes.

It is sweet as
summer.

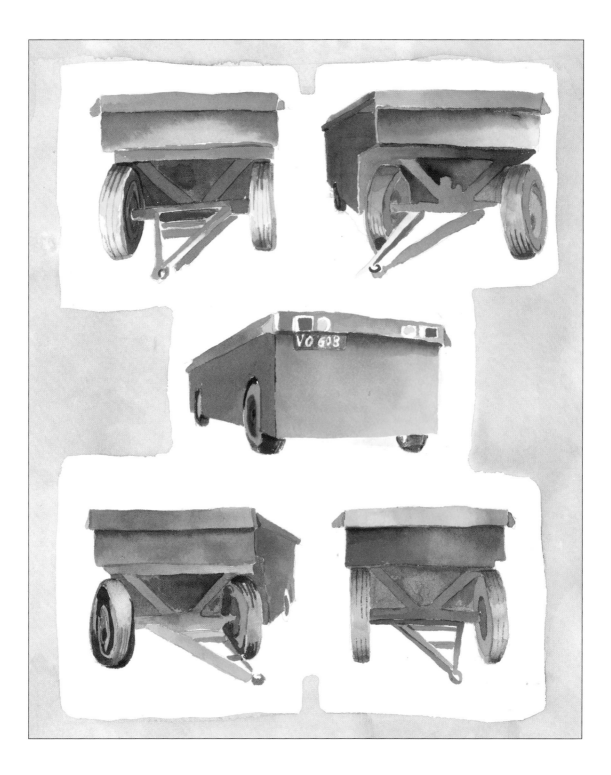

Julian's father arrives with Jenna. Julian shows his sister how to count the gondolas the way Lorenzo has taught him. *"Uno, dos, tres, quatro, cinco,"* he says. "One, two, three, four, five."

The mountain of grapes in the gondola grows. The hot air buzzes with bees, drawn by the ripe grapes' heavy, flowery smell.

Julian's father pulls out the leaves and the twirly pieces of grapevine as the grapes pour into the gondola. "Leaves don't make the wine taste good," he tells Julian.

Lorenzo pours in a binful and Julian spots a big green grasshopper tumbling in with the fruit. A moment later it wriggles out from under the grapes. Julian sticks out his finger and the grasshopper climbs up.

"You wouldn't be good in the wine either," Julian says.

The grasshopper looks at him and bounds away to its hiding place among the vines.

Julian's mother takes Jenna home for a nap. "Jenna's not
big enough yet to work all morning like you," she tells Julian.

When one gondola is full, Julian and his father pull it into
the shade under the walnut trees and drive an empty one out
to the pickers. The tractor motor roars. The hot sun climbs up
the sky. The pickers' knives flash. They are working as fast as
they can go.

The second gondola is nearly full.

Julian's father says, "Julian, run home and tell your mom to call Mac right away!" Julian runs off toward his house, far away at the other end of the long vineyard row.

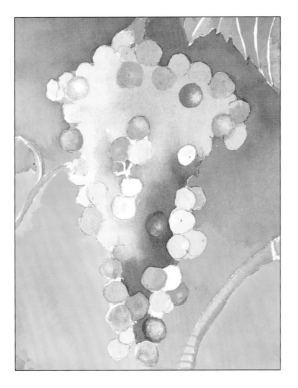

He sees a shiny
bunch of grapes
the pickers missed,
peeking out from
behind some leaves,
but he doesn't stop
to taste.

He sees a jackrabbit bouncing across the vineyard, but he
doesn't stop to watch.

He sees
a lizard
sunbathing
in the dirt, but
he doesn't stop
to catch it.

He runs all the
way.

"Call Mac!" he
tells his mother.
"The grapes are
ready!"

When Mac pulls the
two filled gondolas out
of the gate and off
to the winery, Julian's
father lifts him onto
his shoulders to watch
them rumbling down
the lane.

"Bye," Mac calls.
"See you tomorrow!"

At dinner, Julian and Jenna get cups of juice made from their vineyard's grapes. Their parents drink the new wine from last year's harvest.

"When I was a little girl I helped my father pick grapes in this vineyard," Julian's mother says. "And now Julian's big enough to help us."

"Here's to Julian's first harvest," says his father, raising his glass. He and Julian's mother clink their glasses against Julian's and Jenna's cups, making a sound like tiny bells.

Julian sips. The juice tastes
of the hot sun, the rich earth,
the cool shadows under the leaves
and the ripe sweetness of summer.

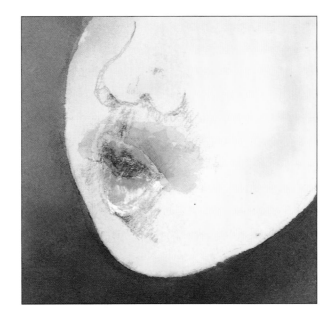

When his father tucks him into
bed, Julian asks sleepily, "Next
year at harvest, will I be big
enough to drive the tractor?"

Julian's father smiles. "No, not
quite big enough yet. But you will
be someday." He points out the
window. "Remember how little the
grapes were last spring, and how
every day they got bigger and
sweeter, until they were so big
and sweet it was time to pick?"

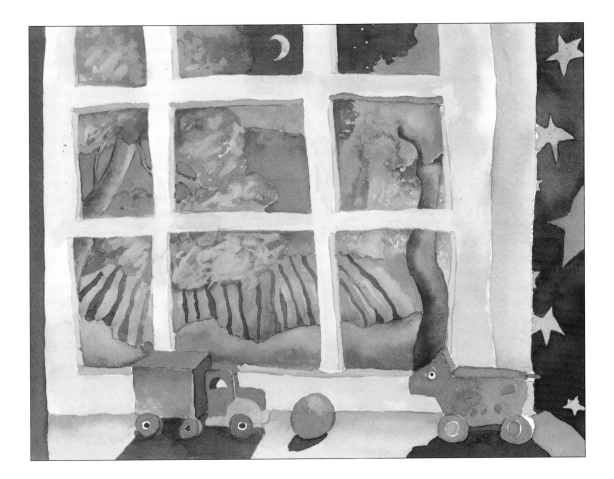

Julian nods. His eyelids are heavy.

"You're growing the same way. Every day you get bigger and stronger. Every year when harvest comes you'll be helping more. Someday you and Jenna will be doing all the work and your mom and I will sit in the shade and watch."

But Julian's eyes have slipped shut.

He is dreaming about grapes and grasshoppers, about gondolas rumbling in the dark and the new sun spreading down the vineyard rows, about Lorenzo's songs and the drowsy buzz of bees.

In his dream the grapes are always sweet and Julian drives the roaring tractor all by himself, all summer long.

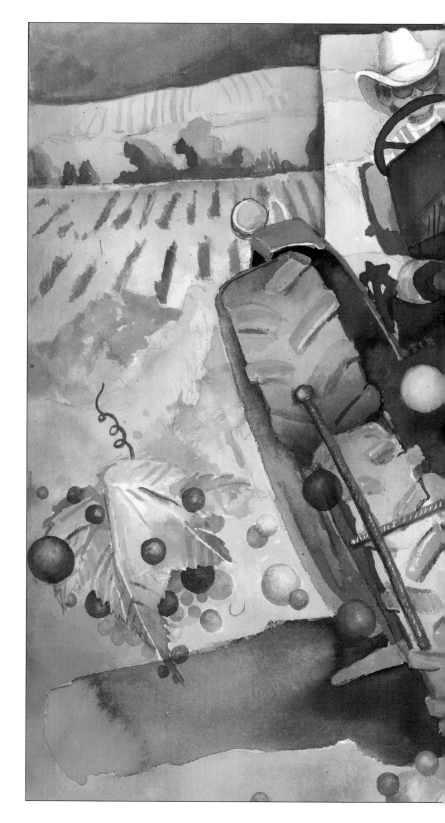

There is a real Julian
who lives in a vineyard
where his father and mother grow grapes,
and where his grandfather and grandmother
and great-grandfather and great-grandmother
grew grapes before them.

The Grapes Grow Sweet

came to life
because of you—

Rosemary Gallagher-Rossi
Barbara Morse
Robin Lewis
and
especially
Wesley Poole

Thank you

Text and Illustrations
© 1996 Lynne Tuft
Printed and Bound in Singapore
by Tien Wah Press

**STUDIO EIGHT
RIVER PRESS**
P. O. Box 5898
Napa, California 94581
(707) 257-8757

Library of Congress Cataloging in Publication Data
Tuft, Lynne and DeCarlo, Tessa
The Grapes Grow Sweet
Summary: A child's first harvest in wine country
Grapes-Fiction, Country Life-Fiction
LC #96-070685
ISBN # 0-9656092-9-4 Hardcover